1912

W9-ASJ-235

ALSO BY SANDRA CISNEROS

Caramelo

Woman Hollering Creek

The House on Mango Street

Loose Woman (poetry)

My Wicked Wicked Ways (poetry)

Hairs/Pelitos (for young readers)

Vintage Cisneros

Have You Seen Marie?

Have You Seen Marie?

Sandra Cisneros

Illustrated by Ester Hernández

Alfred A. Knopf
New York
2012

THIS IS A BORZOI BOOK
PUBLISHED BY ALFRED A. KNOPF
Copyright © 2012 by Sandra Cisneros
Illustrations copyright © 2012 by Ester Hernández
All rights reserved. Published in the United States by Alfred A.
Knopf, a division of Random House, Inc., New York, and in
Canada by Random House of Canada Limited, Toronto.
www.aaknopf.com

Knopf, Borzoi Books, and the colophon are registered trademarks
of Random House, Inc.

Grateful acknowledgment is made to Elena Poniatowska for
permission to reprint an excerpt from *La Flor de Lis*, copyright
© 1998 by Elena Poniatowska. Published by ERA, Mexico DF.
Reprinted by permission of Elena Poniatowska.

Library of Congress Cataloging-in-Publication Data
Cisneros, Sandra.
Have you seen Marie? / by Sandra Cisneros ; illustrated
by Ester Hernández. — 1st ed.
p. cm.
"This is a Borzoi book."
ISBN 978-0-307-59794-6 (hardcover) —
ISBN 978-0-307-96086-3 (ebook)
I. Hernández, Ester, 1944– II. Title.
PS3553.I78H38 2012
813'.54—dc23

2012003532

This is a work of fiction. Names, characters, places, and
incidents either are the product of the author's imagination
or are used fictitiously. Any resemblance to actual persons,
living or dead, events, or locales is entirely coincidental.

Jacket illustration by Ester Hernández
Jacket design by Kelly Blair

Manufactured in Singapore
First Edition

RO426872348

For my brothers,

and . . .

Para aquellos sin madre, ni padre,
ni perro que les ladre.

For those without a mother, without a father,
without even a dog to make a bother.

Es entonces cuando te pregunto, mamá, mi madre, mi
corazón, mi madre, mi corazón, mi madre, mamá, la tristeza
que siento. ¿Ésa dónde la pongo?
¿Dónde, mamá?

It's then I ask you, mama, my mother, my heart, my mother,
my heart, my mother, mama, the sadness I feel. Where do I put it?
Where, mama?

—ELENA PONIATOWSKA,
La Flor de Lis

Have You Seen Marie?

The day Marie and Rosalind
arrived on a visit from Tacoma
was the day Marie ran off.

It had taken three days of driving
to get to San Antonio, and Marie
had cried the whole way.

I felt like crying and taking off, too. My mother had died a few months before. I was fifty-three years old and felt like an orphan.

I *was* an orphan.

Every day I woke up and felt like a glove left behind at the bus station. I didn't know I would feel this way.

Nobody told me.

I'd been hiding in my house since. Most days I didn't even comb my hair, and most days I didn't care. The thought of talking to people made me feel woozy.

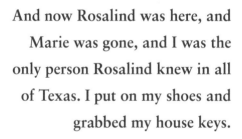

And now Rosalind was here, and Marie was gone, and I was the only person Rosalind knew in all of Texas. I put on my shoes and grabbed my house keys.

★ I followed Roz up and down the streets
of my neighborhood and along both banks
of the San Antonio River.

We asked the neighbors.

We put up flyers. ★

HAVE YOU SEEN MARIE?

★ REWARD ★ RECOMPENSA ★
★ LOST CAT ★ GATA PERDIDA ★
BLACK & BLANCA ★★ WHITE Y NEGRA
She Looks Like She's
Wearing a Tuxedo
CALL /LLAME: 210 555-0107

"Have you seen Marie?"

The Reverend Chavana, who lives in the corner house across the street, said he hadn't seen any new cats around, but he did add as he drove off, "I'll put it on my request list to God!"

"Have you seen Marie?"

Dave, the cowboy next door, came home
for lunch, his truck backfiring like the
Fourth of July, same as always. "We can do
a river search on horseback," he said. "But
my kid is coming over this weekend. Can
you wait till next week?"

"Have you seen Marie?"

My neighbor Carolina came
out to her front gate with her
Yorkie yapping at her feet.

"Oh, my, my, my," she said.
"My heart would break if
I lost my Coco."

She knew about heartbreak
all right. Her brother and
mother had both died within a
year and left her all alone.

"Have you seen Marie?"

Across the street under the shade of a giant pecan tree, the widow Helen sat on the sidewalk doing business with weeds.

"I can't see much of anything till my cataracts are removed," she said. "Would you like a Big Red soda?"

"Have you seen Marie?"

In the blue house that faces mine, Roger and Bill stopped their garden work long enough to read the flyer and shake their heads. Bill had lost his oldest boy a few Thanksgivings ago, and Roger's sister was in the hospital again with cancer. "We haven't seen nothing," they said, but I knew they had seen a lot.

Down the block where Stieren
meets Guenther, a father trimmed
a lantana bush, his two girls hang-
ing upside down from the porch
rail like possums.

★ *"Have you seen Marie?"* ✦

The bigger girl snatched the flyer from her daddy's
hands before he even had a chance to read it.

"How much is the reward?" she asked upside down.
"One hundred dollars," I said, making
up the amount on the spot.

"A hundred dollars!" A boy sailing past in a
bicycle tumbled into the lantana, bike and all.

The smaller girl leapt off the porch rail and took the
flyer over to her cat.

"Muffin, have you seen this kitty?"

Muffin sniffed the flyer,
but did not or would not say.

We walked past the wedding-cake mansions on King William Street and over to the O. Henry footbridge, the iron walkway bouncing and pinging beneath our shoes. Midway we stopped to watch the sky and clouds floating in the water. A jogger mom trotted by pushing a baby in a runner's buggy.

"Have

you

seen . . . "

Our voices echoed off stone and metal.
She was out of sight before we could even finish.

In a hackberry tree shading the Acapulco Ice House, a squirrel flicked her tail like a housewife shaking a dirty dust rag.

"Have you seen Marie?"

The squirrel stared at us suspiciously as if
we'd steal her secret stash of pecans.

"Okay, well . . . Let us know if you
hear something."

We walked down alleys, gravel crunching underfoot.
We talked in between fence slats to folks getting
ready to barbecue, the scent of mesquite and fajitas
reminding us we hadn't had lunch yet.

Over on Adams Street, we interrupted the family
Ozuna's Sunday get-together.

"¿*Qué, qué, qué?*" Grandma Ozuna said.

"They're looking for a cat, Yaya."

"A hat?"

"No, Yaya, *un gato,* a cat. A cat. CAT," they shouted into her ear.

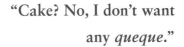

"Cake? No, I don't want any *queque*."

Poor Grandma Ozuna. She'd lost more than a cat, *pobrecita*.

"Marie! Marie!"

We shouted into the muddy crawl space under houses, in the damp chink between garage doors, under peeling plaster and boards loose as rotten teeth. We sent our voices in places too dangerous to go ourselves. Beyond fenced driveways, into dark crannies sticky with cobwebs, between the floor planks of porches, into the mouths of scary hallways. But nothing and no one answered.

On Cedar six bossy Pekingese dogs and one rat terrier with sad, watery eyes threw their bodies against the chain-link fence in a fury.

"Have you seen Marie?"

But they just barked above our voices, except for the rat terrier, who said nothing, too ashamed to disagree with his friends.

At a freshly painted house on South Saint Mary's, an old man in painters' whites pumped my hand and smiled at my teeth. "I lost my wife a while back. Pardon me for asking, but do you have a husband?"

A teenager working at the Ay Tu Car Wash said he hadn't seen our Marie, but asked if we could be on the lookout please for a white cat named Luna. We promised to let him know if we ran into his cat.

Roz and I wedged flyers on doorknobs, tucked them inside the curlicues of gates, clamped them beneath the mousetraps of windshield wipers, stapled them on telephone poles and fences.

We stopped a bearded man in his wheelchair collecting empty cans from the recycling bins of houses on Mission Street. He took our flyer and said, "Man, I'm sorry about your cat. I lost my own cat once and cried like a baby." You only had to look at his faded blue eyes to see that this was probably true.

The neighbor Luli walked
by with her pets following
behind her in single file
like a parade—a cat, a
Chihuahua, and a dog
as fat as a brown bear.
Luli has witnessed too
much grief for one lifetime
and has a teardrop etched near
her left eye to prove it, but, no, she
hadn't seen Marie.

"Isn't it a shame to lose the one you love?"
Luli asked.

"Yes it is," I agreed, and
when I said it,
my heart felt as if someone
squeezed it.

The day grew hot. The top of our heads felt
soft as tar. On San Arturo Street a grandmother watering her thirsty roses told us,
no, she hadn't seen Marie.

"Would you mind watering us please?"
We pointed to our heads.

She did, laughing as she sent a lazy jump
rope of water toward us.

At a lacy Victorian on Barrera Street, we stopped to chat with a woman pretty as a mermaid. She was swinging on a porch swing knitting something purple.

I thought about my mother and how she used to knit ugly scarves no one wanted to wear.

Now I wish I had one of those ugly scarves, and my nose started to tingle.

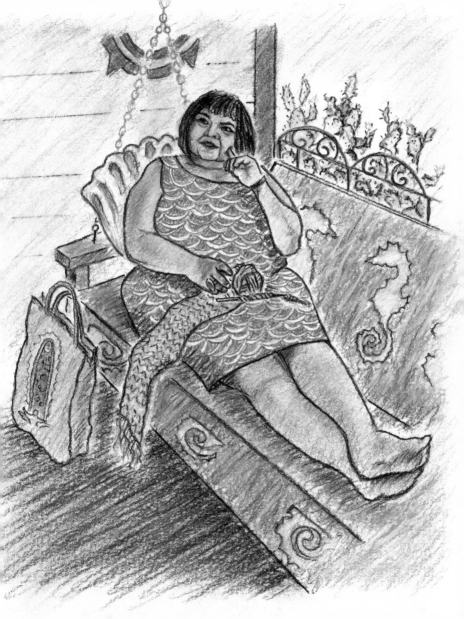

Under the shadow of the Hemisfair tower, at a wooden house off Refugio and Matagorda, a nice couple dining on their porch invited us to look into their bamboo. There was a family of wild cats living there, but the cats wouldn't answer when we asked about Marie, except for a fat gray one with eyes like hubcaps who curled its tail into a question mark. We left with paper plates of brisket, beans, potato salad, and cups of iced tea.

Outside the doors of the Torres Taco Haven,
we caught up with John the mailman, who
knows everything about everything in the
neighborhood. John let his mailbag slide off
his shoulder, readjusted his cap, and then
announced, "Nope. Can't say I've seen any
black-and-white cat . . . But I know a lady over
on Beauregard whose cat just had kittens."

"Have you seen Marie?"

Anne the artist lives next door to the gas station. We found her planting paperwhites in her front yard in memory of her mother. We didn't say much to each other, but that said everything.

"Marie, Marie!"

We called up to trees. We crawled on our hands and knees and peered under parked cars. We walked behind houses and into scratchy, deserted gardens.

But there was no Marie to be found.

At a tiny house on Claudia Street with a
Virgen de Guadalupe *nicho* in the front yard,
silver women in their silver years laughed like bells.

I felt better for a little while.

"May La Virgen look over you, honey bunnies,
and your kitty cat, too."

"Marie, Marie," we shouted.
But, inside, my heart wheezed,
"Mama, Mama."

The sky let out a sigh
and soured into a bruise. Wind
whirled the flyers we had left in
dry hot circles, and big, sad drops
of rain began as if to say,
"Despair, despair."

"Oh, Marie," Rosalind said
out loud, "I miss you."

I said nothing, but swallowed.

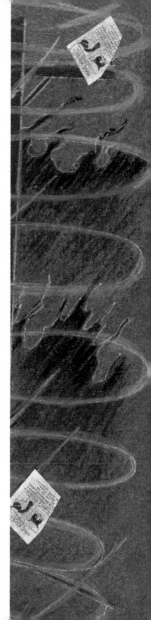

A woman named Beverly called out to us from the corner house on Crofton, the one with the five palm trees. "Hey, I think I've found your Marie!"

"Hallelujah and amen! Bless the Reverend Chavana," Rosalind said.

But when we went to look, it was a big male cat with a white face and black body. Who knew there were so many tuxedo cats in the neighborhood?

"Aw, sweetie," Beverly said, "I'm so sorry," and hugged Rosalind. I felt like asking for a hug, too.

The evening smelled of skunk and jasmine. Rosalind let out a "Have mercy!" We walked and walked and said nothing, our long shadows dawdling behind us as if they were tired.

A house like a black eye,
haunted with rusty vines, a
pickup sagging beneath refrig-
erators. The door opened
a crack and a voice behind a
raggedy screen said, "Can't
help," slamming the door
before we could say what
we came for.

A girl in a fiesta dress and sleeves of tattoos got out of her pickup and said she'd give us her landlord's number so we could look in the back shed. "I have his phone number on a magnet on my fridge. I'll be right back."

She disappeared into the sad apartment house on South Presa, the one with a lightbulb always on, and the front and rear door open like a mountain tunnel. But she never came back, and we didn't know which apartment door to knock on.

Someone sent us to the Cat Lady on Pereida Street across from the Family Dollar store, but there was no one at home except for eleven cats, who looked spooked when we asked about Marie.

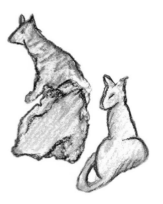

On Wickes Street, my friend Craig came out in his plaid boxers, his pale chest sprouting white hairs, the blue light of the news in the living room, the smell of fried pork chops.

"I'm having my supper, sweetheart. I'll come and help you look later." But later came and went and he forgot.

We consulted with the wise neighbor-lady Blanca on Barbe Street.

"Well, I haven't seen a cat, exactly, but I dreamed just this morning of a black iron fence. Does that mean anything to you?"

We shrugged and said thank you.

Clouds dark and in a hurry swept past. Wind chimes rang. The trees shook their wild, loose hair. Rosalind and I agreed to split up and meet in an hour before it grew too dark to see. Rosalind went upriver toward the flour mill. I went downriver toward the Big Tex granary and the old Lone Star Brewery.

The sun was already behind the freeway.
Grackles gathering in the trees called out,

"Marie? Marie? Marie?"

I asked the river,

"Have you seen Marie?"

River said, *"Mamita,* you name it,
I've seen it."

"Do you mean you've seen her?"

"I've seen everything, *corazón de melón.*
Everything, everything, everything,
everything, everything . . . ,"
River continued.

"But I don't understand what you mean." There was a something in my throat. I felt like I'd swallowed a spoon. I put my face under the water and cried.

River said, "Don't you cry, *mamas*. I will take your tears and carry them to the Texas coast where they'll mix with the salty tears of the Gulf of Mexico, where they will swirl with the waters of the Caribbean, with the wide sea called Sargasso, the water roads of the Atlantic, with the whorls and eddies around the Cape of Good Hope, around that hat called Patagonia, the blue waters of the Black Sea and the pearl-filled waters around the islands of Japan, the coral currents of Java, the rivers of the several continents, the Aegean of Homer's legend, the mighty Amazon, and the wise

Nile, the grandmother and grandfather rivers Tigris and Euphrates, the great mother river the sandy Yangtze, the dancing Danube, and through the strait of the Dardanelles, along the muddy Mekong and the sleepy Ganges, waters warm as soup and waters cold to the teeth, waters carrying away whole villages, waters washing away the dead, and waters bringing new life, the salty and the sweet, mixing with everything, everything, everything, everything."

I raised my face from the water
and shivered.

Along the river there are skunks, raccoons, and possums, snakes and turtles, cormorants, cranes, butterflies, fire ants, and snails. There are hawks in the sky, and beetles in the earth. But no Marie. Timid stars came out one by one and stared at me.

Over at the bend where the river snakes into an *S* there is a muddy puddle. A little underground spring bubbles beneath, feeding into the river. I sat on the giant roots of an ancient Texas cypress wider than thirteen people holding hands, grander than all the fancy mansions in the neighborhood, wiser than any ancient *casita* with its lopsided tin roof, prettier than any house in San Antonio.

A tree so old it had been there since
before Texas was Texas. Since before Tejas
was Tejas. Since before me and my mother.
Since before before.

And when the swirling inside me grew still I heard the voices inside my heart. *I'm afraid. I'm all alone. I have never lived on this earth without you.* Then I really felt sorry for myself and began to shake like branches in rain. *Mother, Ma, Mamaaaá.*

"Here I am, *mija*," the wind said and mussed my hair. "Here I am, *mija*," the trees said and shushed me. "Here I am, *mija*," said the clouds grazing past.

And when the night fell, the moon
rose and blanketed me with her *rebozo* of
stars. "Here I am, I've been here all along,
mijita." "Here, here, here," said the little
stars laughing. "Here I am, here I am." The
light filled my bones.

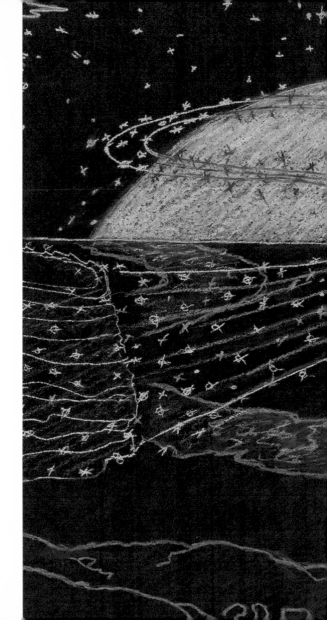

After three days, when her heart was smooth as river stone, Marie came out from under the house where she'd been hiding, and said, "Here I am."

AFTERWORD

In Mexico they say when someone you love dies, a part of you dies with them. But they forget to mention that a part of them is born in you—not immediately, I've learned, but eventually, and gradually. It's an opportunity to be reborn. When you are in between births, there should be some way to indicate to all, "Beware, I am not as I was before. Handle me with care."

I live in San Antonio on the left bank of the river in an area of the city called King William, famous for its historic homes. South of Alamo Street, beyond King William proper, the San Antonio River transforms itself into a wildlife refuge as it makes its way toward the Spanish missions. Behind my house the river is more creek than river. It still has its natural sandy bottom. It hasn't been covered over with concrete yet. Wild animals live in the tall grass and in its waters. My dogs and I can wade across and watch tadpoles and turtles and fish darting about. There are hawks and cranes and owls and other splendid winged creatures in the trees. It is calming and beautiful, especially when you're sad and in need of big doses of beauty.

In the spring after my mother died, a doctor wanted to prescribe pills for depression. "But if I don't feel," I said, "how will I be able to write?" I need to be able to feel things deeply, good or bad, and wade through an emotion to the other shore, toward my rebirth. I knew if I put off moving through grief, the wandering between worlds would only take longer. Even sadness has its place in the universe.

I wish somebody had told me then that death allows you the chance to experience the world soulfully, that the heart is open like the aperture of a camera, taking in everything, painful as well as joyous, sensitive as the skin of water.

I wish somebody had told me to draw near me objects of pure spirit when living between births. My dogs. The trees along the San Antonio River. The sky and clouds reflected in its water. Wind with its scent of spring. Flowers, especially the sympathetic daisy.

I wish somebody had told me love does not die, that we can continue to receive and give love after death. This news is so astonishing to me even now, I wonder why it isn't flashed across the bottom of the television screen on CNN.

I wrote this story in the wake of death—*poco a poco,* slow by slow, little by little. A writer who had come to visit had lost her cat. The real Marie eluded capture for over a week, but searching for her forced me during those days to meet neighbors, and the idea for this book came about.

Some people who heard me perform it out loud thought it was for children, but I wrote it for adults, because something was needed for people like me who suddenly found themselves orphans in midlife. I wanted to be able to make something I could give those who were in mourning, something that would help them find balance again and walk toward their rebirth. Since I've long admired her work, and because she'd recently lost her own mother, too, I knew that the artist Ester Hernández would be right for this collaboration.

Ester flew out from California to San Antonio on a scouting mission. Neighbors and their kids posed for us and got involved in the project: we included real people, houses, and places almost as if we were creating a documentary, and this book became a collective community effort.

I liked the idea of the pictures telling another story about the people of San Antonio, of cultures colliding and creating something new: Folks with blond hair, a German last name, and a Spanish first name inherited from a Mexican grandmother several generations back. Tex-Mexicans with Arab and indigenous features and a Scottish surname. Ultra-devout Catholics with Sephardic roots. Stories the Alamo forgets to remember.

We are a village, of sorts, with big houses and little houses, home to trust-fund babies as well as folks who have to take the bus to buy their groceries. We have houses with American flags and homemade signs. "God Bless Private Manny Cantú." "Bring Home the Troops Now." "Please Don't Let Your Dog Poop On My Yard."

I wanted both the story and the art to capture the offbeat beauty of the *rasquache*, things made with materials readily at hand, funky architecture and funky gardens, creative ways of making do, because it seems to me that this is what is uniquely gorgeous about San Antonio.

I knew as I wrote this story that it was helping to bring me back to myself. It's essential to create when the spirit is dying. It doesn't matter what. Sometimes it helps to draw. Sometimes to plant a garden. Sometimes to make a Valentine's Day card. Or to sing, or create an altar. Creating nourishes the spirit.

I've lived in my neighborhood for over twenty years, longer than I've lived anywhere. Last April, just as folks brushed a new coat of paint on their porches and trimmed their gardens for the annual King William parade, my neighbor, Reverend Chavana, passed away unexpectedly. His family surprised me by asking if I'd write his eulogy. I can't make a casserole, but I felt useful during a time when I usually feel useless, and I was grateful.

There is no getting over death, only learning how to travel alongside it. It knows no linear time. Sometimes the pain is as fresh as if it just happened. Sometimes it's a space I tap with my tongue daily like a missing molar.

Say what they say, some may doubt the existence of God, but everyone is certain of the existence of love. Something is there, then, beyond our lives, that for lack of a better word I'll call spirit. Some know it by other names. I know it only as love.

ACKNOWLEDGMENTS

Thanks to my lovely neighbors and friends who took the time to pose or inspire this story. First and foremost to Rosalind Bell, who lived it. And to Blanca Bolner Bird and her daughter Eleanor, Penny Boyer and Lydia Sánchez, Antonia Castañeda, Theresa E. Chavana and family, David A. Chávez, Josephine F. Garza, Helen G. Geyer, Rodolfo S. López, Carolyn Martínez, Craig Pennel, Gloria Ramírez, William Sánchez, Beverly Schwartzman, John M. Shirley Jr., Roger S. Solís, Brad and Dina Toland and their children Alec and Maddie, Mike Villarreal and Jeanne Russell and their children Bella and Marcos, Anne Wallace, and finally, the real Marie. For allowing me the liberty to imagine your story, I bow with gratitude.

I want to thank *la maestra* Elena Poniatowska for her generosity in allowing me to borrow her words from *La Flor de Lis*.

I am grateful to my Macondo buddies, who serve as my personal editors—Dennis Mathis, Kristin Naca, Erasmo Guerra, and Ruth Béhar. For faith and vision I am blessed with my agent Susan Bergholz and editor Robin Desser. Liliana Valenzuela once again gave light to my work with her own sparkling translation; as ever she did so with a poet's ear, a hummingbird's speed, and the Buddha's patience. Thank you, Olivia Doerge and Irma Carolina Rubio, for your gentle care during my period of grief. Finally, how did I convince Ester Hernández to agree to voyage beyond the zone of comfort? Who knows, but good lucky.

Thank you, San Antonio. *Gracias a la vida.*

—SANDRA CISNEROS

Gracias, Sandra, for being a sister and *comadre* by honoring and entrusting me with the illustrations for your beautiful story—our story, which allowed me to venture into new territories of creativity. For Susan Bergholz, our agent, and Robin Desser, our editor from Knopf, for your respectful support, wisdom, and guidance throughout this book project—my first. To my son Jacobo, daughter-in-law Kazuyo, and granddaughter Anais Yuzuki for your unconditional love and support. To all my other family and friends who were patiently and lovingly behind me when I "disappeared." To all of you who inspired and modeled for us, especially Geri Montano, Michelle Mounton, Ana Guadalupe Avilés, Anais Tsujii Durbin, Luz Medina Hernández, Esperanza López, Sonia (SashaBlue) Martínez, Renee Peña-Govea, Maya Paredes Hernández, and Buzter Chang Chidmat—we couldn't have done it without you . . . thank you for your belief in the book. *Y, gracias a Tonantzin/la Virgen de Guadalupe* and the spirit of my ancestors, I know I am never alone . . .

—ESTER HERNÁNDEZ

Sandra Cisneros was born in Chicago in 1954. She is the author of two novels, the internationally acclaimed *The House on Mango Street,* and *Caramelo,* awarded the Premio Napoli, nominated for the Orange Prize, and shortlisted for the International IMPAC DUBLIN Literary Award.

Her awards include National Endowment of the Arts Fellowships for both fiction and poetry, the Lannan Literary Award, the American Book Award, the Texas Medal of the Arts, and a MacArthur Fellowship.

Other books include the story collection *Woman Hollering Creek;* two books of poetry, *My Wicked Wicked Ways* and *Loose Woman;* and two books of children's literature, *Hairs/Pelitos* and *Bravo, Bruno;* as well as *Vintage Cisneros.* Her work has been translated into more than twenty languages.

Cisneros is the founder of the Alfredo Cisneros Del Moral and the Macondo Foundations, which serve creative writers.

Find her online at www.sandracisneros.com.

Ester Hernández is an internationally acclaimed visual artist best known for her pastels, paintings, and prints of Chicana/Latina women. Her work is in the permanent collections of the Smithsonian American Art Museum, the Library of Congress, the San Francisco Museum of Modern Art, the Mexican Museum in San Francisco, the National Museum of Mexican Art in Chicago, and the Museo Casa Estudio Diego Rivera y Frida Kahlo in Mexico City. Her artistic archives are housed at Stanford University. Born and raised in California, she lives in San Francisco. Find her online at www.esterhernandez.com.

A NOTE ON THE TYPE

The text of this book was set in Sabon, a typeface designed in 1966 by Jan Tschichold (1902–1974). Based on the original designs by Claude Garamond (c. 1480–1561), Sabon was named for the famous Lyons punch cutter Jacques Sabon, who is thought to have brought some of Garamond's matrices to Frankfurt.

Composed by North Market Street Graphics,
Lancaster, Pennsylvania

Printed and bound by Tien Wah Press,
Singapore

Designed by Claudia Martinez